Farmyard Tales Flip Books

The New Pony

Heather Amery

Illustrated by Stephen Cartwright

Language consultant: Betty Root
Series editor: Jenny Tyler

There is a little yellow duck to find on every page.

This is Apple Tree Farm.

This is Mrs. Boot, the farmer. She has two children, called Poppy and Sam, and a dog called Rusty.

Mr. Boot, Poppy and Sam go for a walk.

They see a new pony. "She belongs to Mr. Stone, who's just bought Old Gate Farm," says Mr. Boot.

The pony looks sad.

Her coat is rough and dirty. She looks hungry.
It looks as though no one takes care of her.

Poppy tries to stroke the pony.

"She's not very friendly," says Sam. "Mr. Stone says she's bad tempered," says Mr. Boot.

Poppy feeds the pony.

Every day, Poppy takes her apples and carrots.
But she always stays on the other side of the gate.

One day, Poppy takes Sam with her.

They cannot see the pony anywhere. The field
looks empty. "Where is she?" says Sam.

Poppy and Sam open the gate.

Rusty runs into the field. Poppy and Sam are a
bit scared. "We must find the pony," says Poppy.

"There she is," says Sam.

The pony has caught her head collar in the fence.
She has been eating the grass on the other side.

Poppy and Sam run home to Mr. Boot.

"Please come and help us, Dad," says Poppy. "The pony is caught in the fence. She will hurt herself."

Mr. Boot walks up to the pony.

He unhooks the pony's head collar from the fence.
"She's not hurt," says Mr. Boot.

"The pony's chasing us."

"Quick, run," says Sam. "It's all right," says Poppy, patting the pony. "She just wants to be friends."

They see an angry man. It is Mr. Stone.

"Leave my pony alone," says Mr. Stone. "And get out of my field." He waves his stick at Poppy.

The pony is afraid of Mr. Stone.

Mr. Stone tries to hit the pony with his stick. "I'm going to get rid of that nasty animal," he says.

Poppy grabs his arm.

"You mustn't hit the pony," she cries. "Come on Poppy," says Mr. Boot. "Let's go home."

Next day, there's a surprise for Poppy.

The pony is at Apple Tree Farm. "We've bought her for you," says Mrs. Boot. "Thank you," says Poppy.

"Rusty went with him," says Sam.

"That's why he jumped on the train," says Poppy.
"Clever Rusty," says Sam.

"It's my little Mopp."

Mrs. Hill picks up her puppy. "Poor little thing.
Did you go on the train all by yourself?"

"Come on, Rusty."

"Your ride on the train is over," says Mrs. Boot.
Rusty jumps down. "What's he got?" says Sam.

The train stops at the station.

The fireman climbs down from the engine. He opens the carriage door.

At last, the train comes back.

"Look, there's Rusty," says Sam. "You naughty dog,
where have you been?" says Poppy.

"What shall we do?"

"Both dogs have gone," says Sam. "We'll have to wait for the train to come back," says Mrs. Boot.

"Stop, stop the train," shouts Sam.

Mrs. Boot, Poppy and Sam shout and wave.
But the train puffs away down the track.

"Come back, Rusty," shouts Sam.

Rusty looks out of the window. "There he is," says
Poppy. "He's going for a train ride on his own."

Rusty watches it go.

He pulls and pulls and runs away. Then he jumps
through an open carriage window.

"Where's my puppy?"

"Mopp was with me on the platform," says Mrs. Hill.
"Now he's gone." The train starts to move.

The train is ready to go.

Everyone talks to the train driver. The fireman shuts the doors. He climbs on the train.

They wait on the platform.

Mrs. Boot, Poppy and Sam watch the train come in.
Mrs. Hill and her puppy watch with them.

"Come on, Rusty," says Sam.

They walk down the road to the station. "Don't let Rusty go. Hold him tight," says Mrs. Boot.

They are having breakfast.

"What are we doing today?" says Sam. "Let's go and see the old steam train," says Mrs. Boot.

This is Apple Tree Farm.

This is Mrs. Boot, the farmer. She has two children, called Poppy and Sam, and a dog called Rusty.

Farmyard Tales Flip Books
Rusty's Train Ride

Heather Amery

Illustrated by Stephen Cartwright

Language consultant: Betty Root
Series editor: Jenny Tyler

There is a little yellow duck to find on every page.